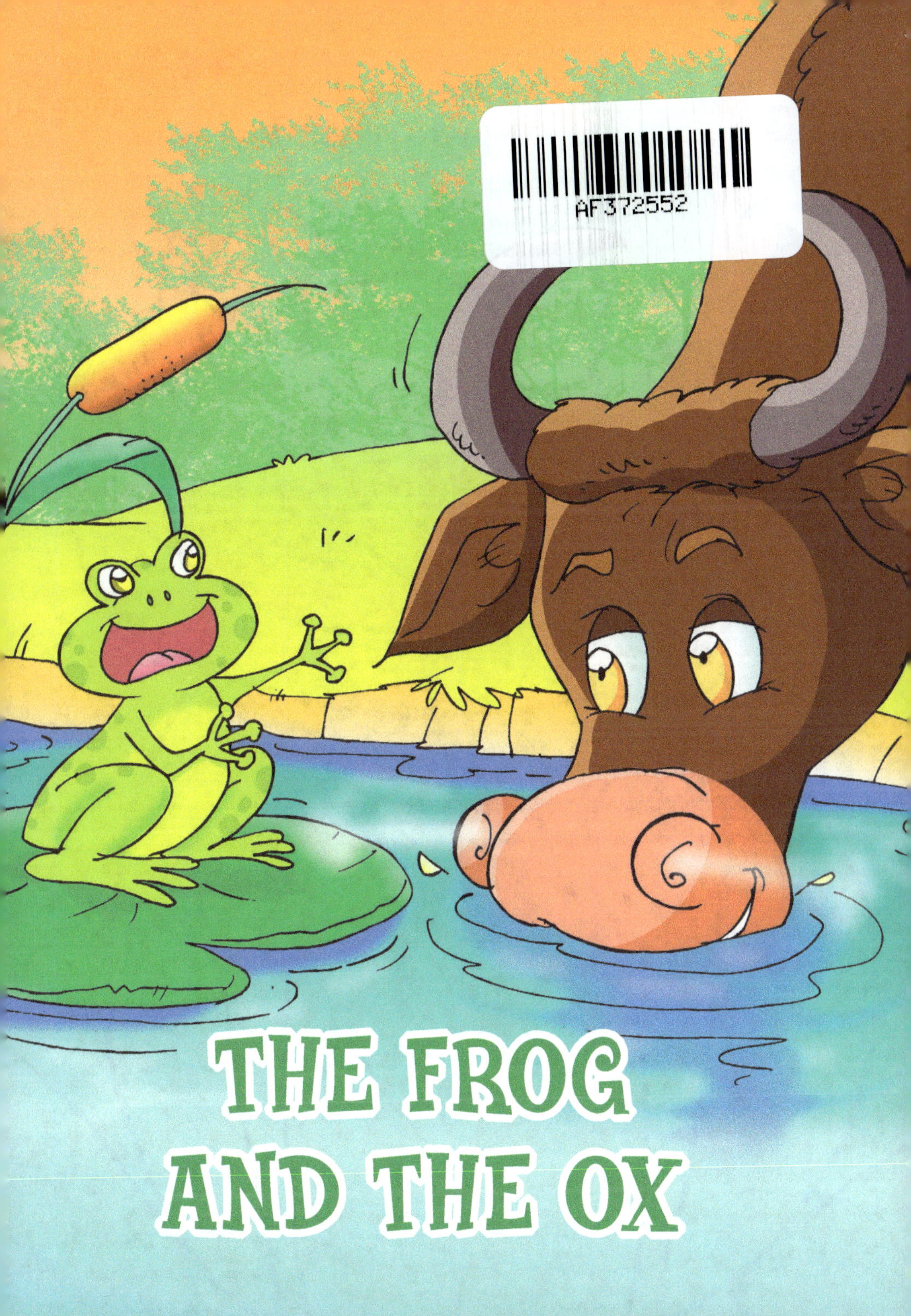

THE FROG
AND THE OX

ONCE UPON A TIME, THERE WAS A VERY SNOBBISH FROG WHO LIVED IN A POND.

HE WAS THE BIGGEST FROG OF ALL AND LOVED TO SHOW OFF HIS SIZE TO HIS FRIENDS.

ONE DAY, AN OX, WHO LIVED ON A FARM NEARBY, WENT TO THE LAKE TO DRINK WATER.

UPON SEEING THE ANIMAL APPROACHING, THE FROG WAS SURPRISED AND A LITTLE FRIGHTENED BY HIS SIZE.

HOWEVER, AS HE DIDN'T WANT TO SHOW FEAR, HE DECIDED TO TELL HIS FRIENDS THAT HE COULD GROW BIGGER THAN THE OX.

THE FRIENDS LAUGHED AT THE FROG, WHO STARTED TO INFLATE TO SHOW THAT HE WAS CAPABLE OF GROWING.

THE OX WAS NOT INTERESTED
IN COMPETITIONS...

...BUT THE FROG BOTHERED HIM SO MUCH THAT HE BECAME VERY ANGRY AND ACCEPTED THE CHALLENGE OF THE LITTLE AMPHIBIAN.

TO BE ABLE TO SHOW OFF AND PROVE
THAT HE COULD GROW...

...THE FROG STARTED TO PUFF UP HIS BELLY
TO TRY TO BECOME THE SIZE OF THE OX.

THE FROG RETURNED TO THE POND AND CONTINUED TO INFLATE, AS HE WANTED TO GROW EVEN MORE.

HOWEVER, THE ONLY THING HE MANAGED TO DO WAS TO PROVOKE LAUGHTER FROM THE OTHER LITTLE FROGS.

THE OX TOLD THE FROG TO GIVE UP ON THAT SILLY COMPETITION, BUT HE DIDN'T WANT TO.

THE MORE THE OX SPOKE, THE MORE
THE FROG INFLATED HIS BELLY.

EVERYONE WAS LOOKING AT
THE FROG, WORRIED.

SUDDENLY, THE FROG BURST ITS BELLY, SURPRISING EVERYONE.

THE END.

www.ingramcontent.com/pod-product-compliance
Lightning Source LLC
Chambersburg PA
CBHW071307130726
47998CB00003B/1369